iVy + bEAN

BOOK 3

ALSO AVAILABLE:

IVY + BEAN BOOK **1**

"The deliciousness is in the details here, with both girls drawn distinctly and with flair."
—★*Booklist*, starred review

". . . illustrations deftly capture the girls' personalities and the tale's humor. . . . Barrows's narrative brims with sprightly dialogue."
—★*Publishers Weekly*, starred review

"Readers are bound to embrace this spunky twosome and eagerly anticipate their continuing tales of mischief and mayhem."
—*Kirkus Reviews*

IVY + BEAN AND THE GHOST THAT HAD TO GO BOOK **2**

"This strong follow-up. . . is sure to please."
—*Kirkus Reviews*

". . . the series' strong suits are humor and the spot-on take on relationships."
—*Booklist*

"This story defies expectations of what an early chapter book can be."
—*School Library Journal*

iVy + BEAN

BREAK THE FOSSIL RECORD

BOOK 3

written by annie barrows + illustrated by sophie blackall

SCHOLASTIC INC.

New York Toronto London Auckland Sydney
Mexico City New Delhi Hong Kong Buenos Aires

For Clio and Esme, who laugh at all the right parts —A. B.

For Georgia and Silas, finders of impressive bones —S. B.

Ping-Pong is a registered trademark of Parker Brothers, Inc.
M&M's is a registered trademark of Mars, Inc.

ISBN-13: 978-0-545-05643-4
ISBN-10: 0-545-05643-8

Text copyright © 2007 by Annie Barrows.
Illustrations copyright © 2007 by Sophie Blackall. All rights reserved.
Published by Scholastic Inc., 557 Broadway, New York, NY 10012, by arrangement with Chronicle Books LLC. SCHOLASTIC and associated logos are trademarks and/or registered trademarks of Scholastic Inc.

17 16 15 14 13 12 11 10 9 8 7 6 5 4 3 2 1   12 13/0

Printed in the U.S.A.   40

First Scholastic printing, January 2008

Series design by Sara Gillingham
Book design by Katie Jennings and Sara Gillingham
Typeset in Candida and Blockhead

The illustrations in this book were rendered in Chinese ink.

CONTENTS

DROP EVERYTHING!

Boring.

Boring!

Boring!

Bean turned her book upside down and tried to read it that way. Cool. Well, sort of cool. No. Boring.

Bean sighed and turned her book back right side up. It was a book about cats that she had picked from the school library. There was a different cat on each page. Bean liked cats, but reading about them was driving her crazy. All the cats looked the same except the sphynx cat, who didn't have any fur. He looked halfway between a dog and a rat. Bean liked him the best.

I bet Ivy's never seen a sphynx cat, thought Bean. She knew she wasn't supposed to talk during Drop Everything and Read, so she poked Ivy in the ribs.

Ivy's eyes were binging across the pages of her book. Bing, bing, bing. She looked like she was watching a Ping-Pong game. She didn't even notice Bean.

So Bean poked her again. "Hey!" she whispered. "Earth to Ivy!"

"Hmm?" Ivy mumbled.

"Looky here! It's a dog-rat!" Bean whispered louder.

Ivy looked for a little tiny second.

"Oh," she said and went back to reading.

Bean sighed again. All the other kids in Ms. Aruba-Tate's second-grade classroom were bent over their books. Even Eric, who usually fell out of his chair two or three times during Drop Everything and Read,

was quiet. He had a book about man-eating
sharks.

MacAdam was picking his nose. Bean
raised her hand. Ms. Aruba-Tate didn't see
because she was reading, too, so Bean called
out, "Ms. Aruba-Tate!"

"Shhh," whispered Ms. Aruba-Tate. "What is it, Bean?"

"There's a problem, and it starts with *M*," began Bean, looking hard at MacAdam. "And then *N* and *P*." She wiggled her finger

next to her nose, just in case Ms. Aruba-Tate needed an extra hint.

Ms. Aruba-Tate looked at MacAdam, too. Then she put down her book and came over to Bean's table.

"I brought this from home especially for you, Bean," she said, holding out a big, shiny book. "See," she pointed at the cover. "It's *The Amazing Book of World Records*. I think you'll like it."

Bean wasn't sure. "What's a world record?"

"When someone does something better or longer or weirder than anyone else in the whole world, that means they've set a world record."

"Weirder?" Bean asked. That sounded interesting.

Ms. Aruba-Tate smiled. "There's a man in here who walked on his hands for eight hundred and seventy miles."

"You mean on his hands and knees? Like a baby?"

"No. Just on his hands. With his feet in the air," said Ms. Aruba-Tate.

"No way."

"Read the book. You'll see." Ms. Aruba-Tate returned to her chair.

Bean opened the shiny cover. On the very first

page, there was a picture of a woman whose black hair trailed behind her like a fancy cape. Bean read that the hair was 19 feet long and that the woman had been growing it since she was 12. Wow, thought Bean. Doesn't it get dirt and bugs in it? Bean turned the page. *Eeeew.* A man was eating a scorpion. *Double-eeeew!* He ate 30 scorpions a day! On the next page was a picture of a boy with
256 straws in

his mouth! What did his mouth look like when there were no straws in it? Big and slobbery, Bean guessed.

"Ivy!" she whispered. "Ivy!"

Ivy's eyes stopped binging back and forth. "What?"

"Check this out!"

CARPET VIPERS, HULA HOOPS, AND TWO MILLION TEETH

"He stuck one hundred and fifty-nine clothespins on his face!" shouted Eric. "Look at him!"

It was recess, but instead of soccer or jump rope or monkey bars, the second-graders were huddled under the play structure. At the center of the circle were Bean and her book. Kids pulled the book back and forth, all trying to look at the pages at the same time.

"Look at her! Ninety-nine hula hoops at once!" Vanessa squeaked. "Around her neck, too!"

"Look at this turnip! It weighs thirty-nine pounds!" said Dusit.

"Gross! I hate turnips," Eric said. "My mom made me eat one once, and I spit it into the heater."

"I hate lima beans," said Dusit.

Bean pulled the book back in her direction. After all, Ms. Aruba-Tate had brought it especially for her. "This guy has had more broken bones than any living human," read Bean. In the picture, he was smiling happily. "He's broken his leg fourteen times."

"On purpose?" asked Emma.

"I guess so," said Bean. "He jumps off of buildings."

Drew slid the book his way. "Hey! This guy collects teeth! He has two million teeth!"

"This is the world's most poisonous snake," read Leo, pointing to another picture. "It's called the carpet viper."

"Does it live in carpets?" asked Zuzu. She looked worried.

"In India and Africa," said Leo. "Not here."

Bean slid the book back her way. "Look, Zuzu! This girl did a hundred and nine cartwheels in a row."

"Let me see that!" Zuzu grabbed the book and looked closely at the picture of a teenage girl in tights. "I bet I could do a hundred and ten."

"Bet you couldn't," said Eric. He grabbed the book from Zuzu and flipped through the pages. "This dude, he ate four hundred M&M's in one minute, it says. That's nothing. I bet I could eat a thousand in one minute if I didn't chew."

"You'd choke," warned Leo.

"No. I've had lots of practice," said Eric.

"Look," said Bean, reaching over Eric's shoulder and flipping pages. "Look at this kid. He's only a kid, and he made a world record for hanging spoons on his face. Fifteen. No glue, either."

"How do they stick?" asked Ivy, looking up from her book.

"I can't tell," Bean said. "Sweat, maybe."

"Why would anyone hang spoons on their face?"

"I don't know, but he made a world record." Bean looked at the picture. The kid was covered with spoons, but he still looked proud and happy because he had set a world record.

"I'm going to do sixteen spoons," said Emma, staring at the picture.

"Hey! I was going to do sixteen!" said Bean. She wanted to set a record and have *her* picture in *The Amazing Book of World Records.* Spoons seemed pretty easy. And, unlike some of the records, spoons didn't hurt.

But now Emma had dibs. Dang.

"I'm going to eat five hundred M&M's in a minute," Eric said.

"Where are you going to get five hundred M&M's?" asked Dusit.

Eric thought for a moment. "My uncle gave me ten dollars for my birthday. My dad said I could spend it on anything I want."

"I'm going to do a hundred and eleven cartwheels," said Zuzu, tucking her pink shirt into her pink pants and reclipping her hair.

"I'm going to see if Ms. Aruba-Tate has any spoons," said Emma.

Emma and Zuzu walked off, looking important.

Bean felt left out. What could she do? She flipped through the pages until she came to a picture of a woman holding a broken glass. What? Was there a record for breaking the most glasses? No—the woman had broken it by singing in a really high voice. "*Ahhhhh,*" sang Bean, but softly.

Ivy was still reading.

"What's that book about, anyway?" asked Bean.

When Ivy looked up, her eyes were shining. "This girl. Mary Anning was her name. She found the first whole ichthyosaur fossil in the world. She was only twelve when she did it, too. She lived near the beach and, one day, she saw a skeleton face in the cliffs. So she dug it out—it took her a long time, and everybody made fun of her, but she didn't

care—and it was an ich-thyosaur! Only nobody knew about dinosaurs then. She also found a plesiosaur and a ptero-dactyl. See? This is her." Ivy showed Bean a picture of a girl in a tall hat. She wasn't very pretty, but she was famous and important.

Bean sighed. She was unfamous and unimportant. There had to be some way she could fix that.

ON YOUR MARK, GET SET, YIKES!

The first 40 straws were easy-peasy. Bean stuck them all in her mouth at once. Then she opened another box of straws. "Uhhhr," she said to Ivy, pointing.

"More? Are you sure?" asked Ivy.

Bean nodded. "Ooo-uwer hihy-eh-uh," she grunted, which meant two hundred fifty-seven.

Ivy pulled a straw out of the box and shoved it into Bean's mouth, but she accidentally shoved too hard, and the straw scraped the back of Bean's throat. "Hhha-*aaak*," choked Bean, and the straws sprayed across the kitchen floor.

Ivy winced. "Sorry."

"Ow." Bean's eyes were watering. She looked at the straws all over the kitchen and thought about Mary Anning. She wasn't a quitter, and neither was Bean. She began to pick up the straws. Ivy helped.

Once again, she shoved 40 straws in her mouth, and, very carefully, Ivy pushed in one more. Forty-one. Forty-two. Forty-three. The girls were working so hard that they didn't hear Bean's dad come into the kitchen. Forty-four.

"Hi, Ivy. Hi—Bean, what have you got in your mouth?" Bean's dad said, staring.

"Awww," said Bean.

"Straws," said Ivy helpfully. "She's breaking a world record."

"Excellent," Bean's dad said, leaning over to see better. "How many does she need to get in there?"

"Two hundred and fifty-seven," said Ivy. She looked at Bean.

Bean nodded.

"How many does she have in now?"

"Forty-four."

Her father didn't say anything, but Bean knew what he was thinking. It was no good. She was never going to get 257 straws in her mouth. Sadly, she pulled the straws out. "I'll never break a world's record." She handed the spitty straws to her father.

"Thanks a lot," said Dad. "Maybe there's a different record you could break."

"Like what?" asked Bean. "I can't walk on my hands."

Bean's dad glanced at the sink. He hadn't washed the breakfast dishes yet. "Why don't you set the record for fast dish washing?" he said, smiling. "That would be a good one."

Bean ran to get the book. There were no

records for fastest dishwasher. "This is going to be a piece of cake," said Bean, looking at the counter piled with plates.

"You could do it slowly and still break the record," said Ivy.

"It'll be better to do it fast," said Bean. "Super-fast. Then no one will ever break my record."

Her father began to look a little worried. "Maybe this isn't a very good idea."

"Dad, every day, you and Mom tell me I have to wash the dishes," said Bean, "and now, when I finally want to, you say it's not a good idea." She shook her head. Grown-ups were so weird.

"Well," said her dad, "okay. But be careful."

What was he talking about? She was always careful. Bean began running nice warm water in the sink. She squirted out a big jet of soap, and mountains of bubbles grew. "Keep your eyes peeled," she said to Ivy. "You'll probably only see a blur."

Bean's father ran his hands through his hair. "Couldn't you grow the longest finger-nails instead?" he asked.

"Takes too long. You're the official time-keeper, Ivy," said Bean as the water gushed. "And Dad, you have to take a picture of me when I'm done. With all the shiny clean plates."

"Sure," said her dad.

"I'm going to do all these plates in five

minutes," said Bean. "Got that? Five minutes."

"Okay," said Ivy, looking at the clock. "On your mark. Get set. Go!"

Bean grabbed a plate and plunged it into the water. Wipe, wipe, wipe. She rinsed it in the next-door sink. Rinse, rinse, rinse. She put it in the dish rack. Okay. Next plate.

Wipe, wipe, wipe.

Rinse, rinse, rinse.

Dish rack.

"How am I doing?"

"One minute gone," said Ivy.

Wow. Bean looked at the pile of plates. She would have to hurry. Quickly, she put two plates in the soap and wiped them. Quickly, she rinsed them. Rack! Again!

Wipe! Rinse! Rack! Again!

Wipe! Rinse! Rack! Again!

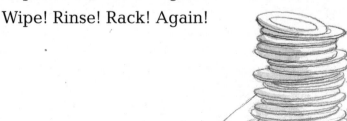

Wipe! Rinse! Rack! Again!

"How many more minutes?" yelled Bean as she scrubbed.

"You've got half a minute left," said Ivy.

"Oh no!" Frantically, Bean took two more plates and plunged them in the soap. Zip, she wiped them. Zip, she put them in the clean water. Dish rack!

"Only ten more seconds!" called Ivy.

There was one more plate left! Bean whizzed it into the soap and shook it. Hurry! She whizzed it into the clean water. Hurry!

"One more second!"

Bean panicked. "YAH!" she screeched, hurling the plate at the dish rack. It flew over the rack and crashed to the floor, shattering into a million pieces.

There was a stunned silence. Ivy, Bean, and Bean's dad stared at the little bits of plate sprinkled over the floor.

Finally, Bean spoke. "Did I do it in five minutes?"

Ivy shook her head. No.

Dang.

WHAT A SCREAM

When Bean's older sister, Nancy, wanted her room painted yellow, Bean's mother said that Bean could pick out a new color for her room, too. Bean picked green. Not light, sweet green. Deep, rich green the color of emeralds. Everyone told her she would get tired of it, but she hadn't. Bean loved her room. It was small and cozy: her bed was in one corner, her toy box in another, her dresser in a third, and, best of all, her basket chair was in the fourth. She liked to sit in her chair and pretend that she was an ape-girl living in a jungle tree house. She had made a lot of pictures of jungle animals and stuck them on the wall. The best was the toucan.

"We could draw," said Ivy, looking at the pictures. "We could draw dinosaurs."

"I don't want to draw. I want to break a world record," said Bean. "Don't you?"

Ivy shrugged. "Not really. Seems like a lot of work for nothing. I don't want spoons all over my face."

"But then you'd be famous," said Bean.

"But I don't care if I'm famous for spoons on my face. If I'm going to be famous, I want to be famous for something important, like Mary Anning."

Bean shook her head. Spoons would be fine with her. But spoons were taken. Bean stared at her green wall and tried to get an idea. Ivy lay down on Bean's bed and tried to imagine finding an ichthyosaur. Quiet minutes went by.

"Hey!" said Bean.

Ivy looked at her.

"I've got a great idea!" said Bean. This was going to be easy. "I'm good at screaming, and I'm good at breaking things, right?"

"I guess so."

"I'll break a glass by screaming," said Bean. "I'll be the youngest person ever to do it."

"What? You scream and throw a glass?" Ivy looked confused. "You already did that with a plate."

"No—the scream breaks the glass. This lady in the book did it.

She screamed so loud that a wine glass shattered. But she was old. I could probably scream louder because I'm young. I'll be a record breaker."

"That's a good record," said Ivy. "That'll be fun." She bounced a little on Bean's bed.

"Okay," said Bean, "I'll need a wine glass. I'll go get it." She jumped up. And then she sat down again. Her dad was still sweeping up little pieces of plate. He probably wouldn't be very happy to find out that she was planning to break something else. Maybe she could find something made of glass upstairs where he wouldn't need to know about it. Not a mirror. That was bad luck. But there had to be something she could use. "I've got it!" she yelled.

"Got what?"

"Nancy's glass animals. I'll shatter one of them. It'll be even better than a wine glass."

"Won't Nancy get mad?"

Bean pictured Nancy's face and then quickly put it out of her mind. "No. She has gazillions of them, and besides, I'll glue the animal back together when I'm done. She won't even notice." I hope, she added silently.

Ivy went on a spying mission down the hall, past Nancy's room.

"The coast is clear," she reported when she came back. "She's not in her room."

"Okeydoke," said Bean. She took a deep breath and headed for the door on super-quiet tiptoe.

Nancy's room was very organized. All her books were neatly arranged by color. Her yarn for knitting was rolled into tight balls. Her friendship bracelets were lying side by side on her dresser. And her glass animals were lined up in two long, straight rows across the top of her bookshelf. It was like a glass-animal army. Nancy had been collecting them since she was five. She had plain china cats and dogs and turtles—the kind that you can get at the drugstore—but she also had some fancy animals, too: tiny dolphins and horses and butterflies. She had

a beautiful unicorn with a blue glass horn, and a peacock made of glass that shimmered like rainbows. Bean wasn't going to hurt *him.* But right in the middle of the army was a gloopy-looking octopus with eight squiggly legs. That was the one, Bean decided. Its legs were thin. They would probably pop right off if she gave a good scream. And they'd be easy to glue back on. Nancy would never have to know.

Bean grabbed the octopus and stuffed it down her shirt, just to be safe. She tiptoed back to her room.

"Got it," she said, setting the octopus on her dresser. She took a few short breaths to get in the mood and looked hard at the little octopus. Its gloopy head dangled on one side. "Prepare to die," she told it and opened her mouth. Then she paused and looked at Ivy. "You might want to cover your ears."

"Okay." Ivy stuck her fingers in her ears.

Bean screamed as loud and high and shattering as she could.

The octopus just sat there. It didn't even crack.

So Bean screamed again, louder than she had ever screamed before. But even through her scream, Bean could hear another sound. It was the sound of her father running up the stairs, very, very fast.

A second later, he burst through the door. "What?! What's the matter?!" he shouted. His face was whitish gray.

Bean stopped screaming. "Nothing," she said. "What's the matter with *you?*"

WATCH YOUR TAIL, MARY ANNING

It was cold outside. The two girls squished into Bean's tiny playhouse.

"How long do we have to stay out here?" asked Ivy.

"I don't know. He said until dinner, but I don't think he meant it." Bean sighed. She knew he meant it. "Is your mom home?"

"Not yet, I don't think."

"Bummer."

"He'll let us in if it starts raining, won't he?"

"Yeah, but I don't think it's going to rain," said Bean, peering out the bitty window at the sky.

"Mary Anning used to go out hunting for fossils in storms. She didn't mind," said Ivy. "She built her own wooden tower next to the cliff where she saw the skeleton, and she lay down on it and chipped the ichthyosaur out of the cliff even though the tower was shaking and the rain was pouring down on her."

"Why didn't she just wait until it stopped raining?" asked Bean.

"She was afraid that the bones would get washed away in the storm," explained Ivy.

"Wow." Bean pictured herself lying bravely on top of a shaking wooden tower with rain falling in her eyes.

"It took her a year to get the whole body out," Ivy added. "Chip, chip, chip, a tiny bit at a time."

"A *year!*" yelped Bean. "Didn't she get bored out of her mind?"

"No," said Ivy. "It takes a lot of patience to dig up fossils." She sat up and peered out the other bitty window of the playhouse. "Dinosaurs lived all over, you know."

"I know."

"There were dinosaurs around here, too. Not ichthyosaurs, but other kinds."

"Maybe just little ones," said Bean.

"Maybe just little ones," said Ivy. "But still, dinosaurs."

"I've always liked those little ones with the deadly claws," said Bean.

"Mary Anning found fossils right on the top of the ground, but sometimes they're buried deep in the dirt. We might have to dig for a long time before we find one."

"That's okay. We're patient," said Bean. She was beginning to get it.

"Where do you keep your shovels?" said Ivy.

Bean loved to dig. Her shovel flashed, and dirt flew through the air. Soon, there was a nice, wide hole next to the trampoline. Ivy knelt beside it and ran her fingers through the dirt.

"We have to inspect every bit of it," Ivy said. "Even slivers of bone are important to paleontologists."

"What's that?"

"That's us," said Ivy. "The people who dig up dinosaurs are called paleontologists."

"Cool." Bean felt cheerful. She loved the crunch of her shovel as it went into the earth. She loved hurling the dirt behind her without looking. Whee!

"Hey, watch out! You got dirt in my hair!" cried Ivy.

"We're paleontologists! We can't be afraid of a little dirt!" yelled Bean. The hole was almost 2 feet deep, and the dirt was getting darker and wetter. She flung a big hunk of it over her shoulder.

"Ouch!" Something bounced off of Ivy's head and landed next to her knee. She picked it up, brushing away the mud that was stuck to it. What was it?

It was about as long as her hand.

It was narrow at one end and flared out at the other.

It was grayish brown.

It was a bone.

"Bean!" Ivy gasped. "Lookit! I got one."

Bean's shovel crashed to the ground, and she rushed to Ivy's side. Ivy

handed her the gray brown bone. Bean stared at it and then gave a long whistle. "Watch your tail, Mary Anning!" she said. "Here we come."

IVYBEANOSAUR

They dug for half an hour without finding any more bones. Bean was on the edge of giving up. She figured that one bone was a lot more than most people found. But then she thought of Mary Anning chip, chip, chipping for a year. She didn't want to be wimpier than Mary Anning. Or Ivy. So she dug and dug.

Ivy's nose was running, and she had mud all over her. Also, her feet had gone to sleep from being kneeled on. But she didn't give up either. She combed through each new load of dirt with her fingers, feeling for bones. She found a lot of rocks. She found a marble. She found a piece of blue plastic.

Then her fingers, burrowing into the mud like worms, plucked out another bone. This one was shorter and thicker, but it was definitely a bone. "I got another one!" she called. Bean dropped down beside her and looked at the gray brown lump.

"We rock," she said.

"No. We fossil," giggled Ivy. She dusted the bone carefully and put it next to the first one. "We can put them together later," she said.

"How do you put them together if you don't know which dinosaur it is?" asked Bean.

"It's like a puzzle, I think. You look for pieces that fit together," said Ivy. "We can look in dinosaur books, too, so it's a lot easier for us than for Mary Anning. She didn't have any pictures to look at. But," she remembered, "Mary Anning found the whole ichthyosaur, so she didn't need to put it together."

"It's sort of cheating to find the whole thing," said Bean. "Oh man! Here's a big one!" She fished around in the dirt and pulled out a thick, heavy bone. It was a very serious-looking bone. Bean held it up. It reached from her hand to her elbow. She whistled. "This is no little, cute dinosaur. This is a big, scary dinosaur."

"What if that's just its little finger?" said Ivy dreamily.

"Monsterosaur!" said Bean.

"IvyBeanosaur!" said Ivy. "You're supposed to name them after the person who discovered them."

Bean giggled. Then her shovel hit something hard. Another bone appeared, this one smooth and rounded. "Whoa, Nellie!"

cried Bean. "I think I got a piece of its skull!"

A few minutes later, Bean found another small bone. Ivy found two more—one big, the other medium. There was no doubt about it: The backyard had been swarming with dinosaurs.

"You know," Ivy said, holding up her ninth bone. (They didn't even call out when they found them now.) "Mary Anning was *twelve* when she found her ichthyosaur. We're only seven. We're probably the youngest paleontologists in the world."

Bean stopped digging and leaned on her shovel. The youngest paleontologists in the world? "Ivy, you know what that means?"

"Huh?"

"It means we're record breakers!"

Ivy stopped rubbing dirt. She and Bean grinned at each other. "Youngest paleontologists in the world," said Ivy. "That's way better than spoons."

By the time Ivy had to go home, the girls had found 17 bones. They were all different sizes, but they were clearly from the same dinosaur because they were all the same shade of grayish brown.

Bean's father called her in for dinner. Bean washed off most of the dirt and sat down at the dining room table. She smiled, thinking about the dinosaur skeleton she and Ivy were going to build. They were totally awesome. They would probably be on TV. Her parents would have to let her watch TV if she was *on* it. Bean noticed that Nancy was sneering at her. She was still mad about the octopus.

"If I ever catch you *looking* at one of my glass animals again, you'll be sorry," Nancy hissed while their father served up their pasta.

"What am I supposed to do—put a blindfold on when I go into your room?"

"You're not supposed to go into my room,"

said Nancy. "Because it's *my* room. Daddy, can I get a lock on my door?"

"No," said Dad, bringing in their bowls.

Bean stared at her pasta. It looked funny, but she decided not to say so.

"This pasta looks weird," said Nancy.

"That's what I thought, but I didn't say it," said Bean. "Mom says if you can't say something nice about your food, you shouldn't say anything at all."

Nancy lifted one eyebrow and said, "Little children who break dishes, steal other people's stuff, and screech their brains out have no right to talk about what other people do."

"How about if we don't talk at all for a little while?" suggested Dad.

"Fine with me," said Nancy.

"Me, too," said Bean. So she didn't tell them anything about the amazing dinosaur find in

the backyard. Serves them right, she thought. I'll be the youngest paleontologist in the world, and they won't even know it.

BELIEVE IT OR NOT

"Breaking a world record is harder than it looks," said Emma the next day at recess. The second-graders who had gathered around *The Amazing Book of World Records* the day before were huddled under the play structure again. Without the book. "I could get two spoons stuck on my cheeks, no problem," Emma went on, "and for a second, I got three. But that's all. I wish the book said how that kid did it."

"Did you try your nose?" asked Drew.

"Sure I tried my nose," Emma said. "It slid right off."

"Maybe he has a very sticky face," said Ivy. "Maybe he even puts something on his face to make it sticky."

"Maybe," said Emma, "but forget it. I'm tired of trying to put spoons on my face."

There was a silence. Bean didn't want to be a braggy kid. Everyone hates braggy kids. She would wait to tell about the dinosaur bones until someone else told about breaking a record. "How'd the cartwheels go?" she asked Zuzu.

"Super-great," said Zuzu.

"You did it?" asked Ivy. "A hundred and eleven cartwheels?"

Everyone looked impressed. "Wow!" "That's great!" "Are you going to be in the book?"

Zuzu pulled the zipper on her jacket down and up. "I didn't do a hundred and eleven cartwheels. I did thirty-two." She looked around at the faces watching her. "That's a *lot.* I set the record for Emerson School, for sure."

There was a short silence while everyone thought about that. Then Bean said, "Did you fall down or what?"

"I crashed into the fence," said Zuzu. "Got a bunch of splinters."

She held up her knee. It looked like she had pepper under her skin.

"Ouch," said Ivy. She hated splinters.

"If my backyard was a mile long, I bet I could have done it," said Zuzu.

"Eric's not at school today," said Vanessa. "I wonder if he ate five hundred M&M's."

"He didn't," said Dusit. "He ate a hundred and twelve, and then he threw up."

"But a hundred and twelve is hardly anything."

"He didn't chew," said Dusit. "He just poured them down his throat."

"Yuck," said Emma. "That's gross."

"His mom is really mad," said Dusit glumly. "She took the rest of his money away."

"What about you, Bean?" asked Vanessa. "Did you get all those straws in your mouth?"

"Straws?" Bean had almost forgotten the straws. "Oh. No. But Ivy and I broke another record—"

"How many did you get in?" asked Zuzu.

"What? Oh. Forty-four. But guys," said Bean, "Ivy and I broke another record yesterday afternoon." She stopped and waited.

"Well?" said Vanessa. "What record?"

"We became the youngest paleontologists in the world!"

There was a little pause.

"What's a paleontologist?" asked Drew.

"A person who digs up dinosaur bones," said Bean. "And that's what we did! We dug seventeen dinosaur bones out of my backyard yesterday. And today we're going to get more. And then we're going to put them together and make a dinosaur skeleton!"

Nobody said anything.

"Isn't that cool?" said Bean. What was the matter with them?

"You did not," said Dusit, finally.

"We did too!" cried Bean.

"Seventeen dinosaur bones? No way," said Emma.

"Yes way," said Bean firmly.

Zuzu and Emma gave each other a look. Bean felt her face get hot.

"People don't just find dinosaur bones," said Vanessa in a grown-up voice. "Dinosaur bones aren't just lying around."

"Sometimes they are," said Ivy. "That's how Mary Anning found them."

"Until yesterday, Mary Anning was the youngest paleontologist in the world," said Bean, trying again. "Now Ivy and I are."

"You can't just *say* you broke a record and get in the book," said Vanessa. "You have to *prove* it."

"We can prove it," said Ivy. Her face was getting a little pink, too. "We have the bones!"

"How do we know that they're not chicken bones you stuck in the ground yourself?" Vanessa said.

"They're not chicken bones. They're big. You can come over and see them if you don't believe us," said Bean.

"Okay," said Vanessa. "I will."

"In fact, you can all come over," said Bean. "I invite you all over for a dinosaur-bone viewing. So there."

"Fine. When?" said Emma.

"You can come this afternoon." Bean decided. "But don't come early, because Ivy and I have paleontology to do."

"You'd better come and see them today," said Ivy. "When they're in the museum, you'll have to pay! Come on, Bean." They turned their backs on the play structure and walked toward the classroom.

A BONE TO PICK

Bean could hardly wait for the end of the day. Finally, Ms. Aruba-Tate said, "Put up your chairs, boys and girls," just like she always did. Bean and Ivy put up their chairs—*wham, wham*—and hurried out of the classroom.

"Wait, you guys!" Leo ran down the breezeway and stood in front of them.

They waited.

"Did you really?" he said.

"What?" said Ivy in a huffy voice.

"Find dinosaur bones?" He looked at them with narrow eyes.

Bean's face got hot again. Leo was their friend, and friends believed you. He shouldn't think they were lying. It made her mad. "Yes! We did!" she yelled. "And we have proof! Anyone who doesn't believe us can come over and see! Four o'clock! Today! My house! Dinosaurs!" She glared at Leo. "Bring everyone you know! Bring your stupid soccer team! I don't care!"

"Jeez," said Leo. "Lighten up."

"Excuse me," said Ivy, still in a huffy voice. "We have work to do." She pulled Bean by the arm.

A skinny first-grader plucked at her jacket when she reached the stairs. "I heard you found dinosaur bones," he said.

"Yes, we did," said Bean in a loud voice. "We found dinosaur bones."

He looked at her nervously. "Can I see them?"

"Oh." Bean had been ready for a fight. She tried to make her face into a smile as she told the kid where she lived. "Come by later this afternoon," she said.

"Okay," he smiled. "Can I bring my mom?"

"Bring anyone you want."

As they walked home, Ivy said, "Nobody believed Mary Anning, either. They thought that the bones were just weird rocks. They told her to stop wasting her time. But in the end, she was right. Who cares what other people think?"

Bean stepped over a crack in the sidewalk. "I do. I want other people to know I'm right. Especially when I really *am* right."

Ivy thought for a moment. "But you're still right, even if they don't think so."

"I guess." Bean sighed. "I just feel better if other people think I'm right, too."

"Hardly anybody ever thinks I'm right," said Ivy.

Bean nodded. That was true. A lot of people didn't understand Ivy's ideas. She had had plenty of practice at not being believed. That's probably why she didn't get as mad about it as Bean did. She just went ahead with her ideas anyway. You can do whatever you want if you don't care what people think, Bean realized. But you have to do it alone a lot of the time.

They climbed the stairs to Bean's front porch. "We need a good snack," said Bean. "We have lots of digging to do."

"A great big snack," agreed Ivy. "What do you have?"

"Trail mix," said Bean. "The kind with chocolate chips."

"Cool. We can eat it while we dig."

"We should be kind of quiet," Bean added. "I think my dad is still a little grumpy from yesterday."

But he wasn't. He was standing in the front hall with a big smile on his face. "Hi, girls!" he called out. "How was school? Learn anything good? What's two plus two? Eight?"

Bean giggled. Sometimes her dad was a goofball. "Four," she said.

"Wrong again!" He slapped his head. "You want a snack? I made banana bread."

"You did? How come?" Bean said.

"Because I make great banana bread. Duh," he said, bustling toward the kitchen.

He was awfully cheerful. Bean put her

hands on her hips. "What's going on around here, Dad? Why are you so happy?"

Dad stopped bustling toward the kitchen. "I'm glad to see you," he said.

Bean looked at him.

"I *am*." Then he said, "It was quiet around here today."

"Mom says it's peaceful when we're gone," said Bean.

"I don't like peaceful. I was lonely," her dad admitted.

Bean laughed. "Hey. You're just like me."

Her dad had been so lonely that he had made three loaves of banana bread. He cut two thick slices and poured two glasses of milk and brought them to the kitchen table. Then he sat down to watch Bean and Ivy eat.

"What are you guys up to this afternoon?" he asked.

The girls exchanged glances. "It's a secret," said Bean slowly. If she told him, he might want to help, and that would ruin the youngest paleontologist record. He was old. "But by the end of the afternoon, you'll know."

"The end of the afternoon?" He looked disappointed. "Oh."

Ivy felt sorry for him. "Thanks for the banana bread," she said. "It was delicious."

"You're welcome." He picked up the newspaper.

"See you later," said Bean, getting up. She stopped and turned back to the table. "There might be some kids coming over later," she said. "Just in the yard."

He was reading.

"Kids. Great," he said.

DORKOSAURUS

"I think we better stop now. We've got to start putting them together," Ivy said.

"Okay." Bean's arms were tired anyway. "We can always dig up more later." There seemed to be no end to the bones in the ground. They had found four more since they had begun. The bone pile was getting high.

Both girls stared at it.

"Hmm," said Ivy.

"Hmm," said Bean.

"They never talk about this part in books," said Ivy. "Should we lay them out and see what fits? That's how you do puzzles."

"Sure, okay," said Bean. "There's some clean grass over there."

Lying out on the grass, the 21 bones didn't look much like a dinosaur. It didn't look much like anything.

"Maybe it's just one part of a dinosaur," said Bean.

"Or maybe it's a small dinosaur," said Ivy. "Remember, the small ones were more common."

"Right."

Ivy picked up the rounded piece that Bean had found the day before. "Let's start with this. It's a piece of skull." She put it down on the ground, apart from the other bones. "So now we have to find a neck."

Bean picked up the long, thick bone. "I bet this is a neck."

Ivy tilted her head to one side as she looked at it. "I think you're right."

This was fun. "Oh, the neck bone's connected to the shoulder bone," sang Bean. Ivy put down a small bone that was almost the shape of a shoulder. "And the shoulder bone's connected to the arm bone! There it is!" Ivy put down a narrow bone. "And the arm bone's connected to the hand bone!"

"They didn't have hands!" Ivy giggled. "How about the backbone?"

"Okay, the backbone."

Ivy put down the first bone they had found. It flared out at one end. "That's the hip," said Ivy.

"Right," said Bean. Then she sang, "The hip bone's connected to the leg bone."

Piece by piece, they made a dinosaur. It was a small dinosaur, and some parts of it were missing, but they would probably find those the next time they dug. When they had it all arranged, they stood back to look at it.

"Pretty good," said Ivy.

"Don't you think we should stick it together?"

"Yeah. I think they do it with wire in museums. Do you have any wire?"

"Wire? I don't think so," said Bean.

Ivy thought for a minute. "Just for now, we could use tape. We can take it off when we get some wire."

"Tape. You got it." Bean ran inside. "I think

it's almost three-thirty," she said when she came out. In-betweens were hard. She was only positive when it was exactly an o'clock.

"This won't take long," Ivy said, pulling out a long piece of tape. She wrapped it around the skull and connected the other end to the neck bone. She had to wrap it four times before it stuck. Bean began to work on the foot. It only had one foot.

They were working so hard that they didn't see Nancy until she was standing right next to them. "That's disgusting," she said, staring at their dinosaur.

Bean jumped. For some reason, she didn't want Nancy to know about the

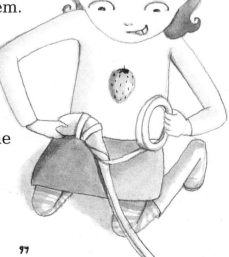

dinosaur. "Go away!" she said.

"What *is* that?" Nancy asked.

Bean would never have answered in a million years, but Ivy didn't know about sisters.

"It's a dinosaur," she said. "A *compsognathus*, I think."

"A dinosaur?" Nancy began to laugh a high, mean laugh. "You think that's a dinosaur?"

"Bug off, potato face!" yelled Bean. She was getting a bad feeling.

"It's a dorkosaurus!" squealed Nancy. She held her stomach like it hurt from laughing. Bean glared at her. "You guys are total losers. A dog buried those. The people who lived here before us had a dog! Look—" she pointed at the neck bone— "That's a steak bone!"

"Get out of here!" shouted Bean. She looked around wildly for something to throw at her.

"Don't worry. I'm leaving," said Nancy, smiling. "Wait till I tell Dad. He's going to be mad that you dug up the yard." She stood on the back porch and made an L-for-loser sign with her finger and thumb.

"Shut up!" screamed Bean. She looked over at Ivy. Ivy was just sitting in the dirt. Bean stared at the dinosaur. Dog bones? Is that why they were so easy to find? Bean felt heavy all of a sudden. She wasn't the youngest paleontologist in the world any more. Mary Anning still had the record. And

Bean had nothing.

"Maybe she's wrong," said Ivy, finally.

"Maybe," said Bean. Somehow, she didn't feel very hopeful.

The back door opened, and Bean looked up, ready to shout at Nancy. But it wasn't Nancy. It was her dad.

He came down the stairs slowly, looking at the hole and the dirt pile and the bones. Then

he looked at Bean and Ivy, sitting quietly on the ground.

"Are you mad about the hole?" Bean asked.

"No. The hole's fine," he said. He squatted down next to her and looked at the dinosaur they had taped together.

"Nancy says they're dog bones," said Bean.

He nodded.

"Are they?" asked Bean.

"I don't know," he said. "They might be."

"Could they be dinosaur bones?" asked Ivy.

"I don't think so," he said slowly. "I'm pretty sure that if there were dinosaur bones here, they'd be buried deeper in the ground. I see that you worked really hard, though."

"Yeah," said Bean. She felt like crying.

There was a knock on the backyard gate.

"Who's that?" asked Bean's dad.

"Everybody," said Ivy glumly.

THE BONES OF MYSTERY

"BEEE-EEEN! IIIII-VEEE!" squalled a voice. "Open the gate!"

I'm going to have to run away, thought Bean. She stood up, preparing for takeoff.

"Open up, you guys!" That was Leo. "I'm going to be late for practice!"

"I'm running away," said Bean. "It was nice knowing you," she said to her dad.

"Wait a second," said Ivy. She looked at Bean's dad. "You don't know what these are the bones of, do you?"

"Nope. Can't say I do," he said.

"So you're saying these bones are pretty mysterious, aren't you?" asked Ivy.

"Sure. They're pretty mysterious."

"The most mysterious bones you've ever seen?"

He smiled. "You bet."

Ivy nodded. "Good."

"BEEEE-EEN!"

Ivy turned to Bean. "Don't worry. It's going to be okay." She walked calmly toward the back gate and opened it.

People streamed in. Bean couldn't believe how many there were. Vanessa, Drew, Dusit, Emma, Zuzu, Sophie W. and Sophie S., Marco, Anya, Nascim, Jared, Leo with five guys she didn't know, Leo's sister Kiki, Isaiah, two fourth-grade girls who Bean didn't know the names of, Leann from down the street, the skinny little first-grader along with about

six other skinny little first-graders, some tiny brothers and sisters, and assorted moms.

"Hi," said Bean in a small voice. What was she going to say to all these people?

"What happens next?" Bean's dad whispered in her ear.

"I don't know," said Bean nervously. The tiny kids started playing in Bean's playhouse, and the moms stood around the edges of the yard looking like they were late for something else, but the big kids crowded around Ivy and Bean. They didn't look really friendly.

"So—let's see the dinosaur bones," said Vanessa.

"Yeah!" squeaked the skinny first-grader. Showtime.

Then Bean heard Ivy take a deep breath. "Attention, please!" Ivy called. She climbed up onto the trampoline and stood there, looking down at everyone. "I have an announcement!"

"What?" said Leo.

Not even Mary Anning was as brave as Ivy, Bean thought. She felt suddenly lighter.

The crowd grew quiet, watching Ivy. She cleared her throat. "This afternoon, we had a visit from an expert, and he told us that these," Ivy pointed to the bones, "are not, I repeat NOT, dinosaur bones." She looked at the crowd below her. "The expert was unable to identify these bones. He says these are the most mysterious bones he has ever seen. Because of that, he has decided to name them The Bones of Mystery."

Wow. Bones of Mystery. That's exactly what they were! Bean climbed onto the trampoline and stood beside Ivy. "These are the bones of a creature never before seen," she said in a loud voice. "Possibly a man-eating, saber-toothed, deadly-clawed creature."

"We will let you know what the creature is as soon as studies have been done," said Ivy. "We regret any inconvenience."

There was a silence. Ivy and Bean looked

down at the kids standing around the trampoline. They looked back. Finally, the skinny first-grader said, "Can I touch The Bones of Mystery?"

"You may," said Bean, feeling like a queen. Kids quickly clustered around the bones, inspecting them and fingering their dirty dryness.

Then Bean's dad spoke up. "I have an announcement, too," he said. "Banana bread will be served in just a moment. Guests are invited to jump on the trampoline in the meantime."

"Cool!" said Dusit, dropping his bone. "Lemme up there!"

"Me, too!" yelled Emma. "I bet I can do a flip."

"So can I," said Zuzu.

There was a rush for the trampoline. Ivy and Bean climbed down to let the others up. Vanessa stood nearby. "I told you they weren't dinosaur bones," she said.

Bean sucked in her breath. She knew what she had to say. "You were right, and we were wrong," she said. "Probably."

"I think it's pretty exciting to find a creature that's never before been seen," said Ivy. "Especially a saber-toothed one."

"Have some banana bread," said Bean's dad, coming up to them with a plate piled high.

"Thanks," said Vanessa. She took two pieces.

Leo was poking the bones with his foot. "Bones of Mystery," he said. "You guys are wacko."

Ivy and Bean looked at each other. "That's what they said about Mary Anning."

ANOTHER DAY, ANOTHER RECORD

The banana bread ran out quickly, but nobody left. Kids were digging and jumping and running around. The first-graders were spraying the hose into Bean's hole. The moms were standing in a circle, chatting.

Bean found her dad sitting on the stairs. "Will you go get your camera?" she asked. "Please?"

He put his arm around her. "Why?"

"I think I'm breaking a record," Bean said.

"Oh yeah? What record?"

"Biggest playdate ever. Come on, go get the camera. You have to have proof." Bean gave him a shove.

"Okay, okay." He got up and went inside.

Ivy climbed the stairs and sat next to her. "I'm still bummed that they aren't dinosaur bones," she said.

"Yeah," Bean said. She was still bummed, too. She had really wanted to be the youngest paleontologist in the world. She looked out over the backyard full of kids. Maybe it wasn't going to be the biggest playdate in the world, either. She should probably have a backup.

"I think I should try to break glass by screaming again. A wine glass. Not an animal."

Ivy nodded. "A wine glass would be easier."

"I'm going to do it. Tomorrow."

Bean's dad came back out on the porch

with the camera. "What are you going to do tomorrow?" he asked.

Bean and Ivy smiled at each other. "Never mind," said Bean.

The End.

ANNIE BARROWS has never even come close to breaking a world record. She can't walk on her hands, she doesn't eat metal, and she has only the regular number of toes. Annie lives in Northern California with her husband and two daughters, all of whom have only the regular number of toes, too. To learn more about Annie and about Ivy and Bean, visit www.anniebarrows.com.

SOPHIE BLACKALL is an Australian illustrator whose work has appeared in many newspapers and magazines, including *The New York Times*. She lives in Brooklyn, New York, with her two delightful, scheming children. Her previous books include *Ruby's Wish* and *Meet Wild Boars*. To learn more about Sophie Blackall, visit www.sophieblackall.com.